If I had a pig

If I had a pig

MICK INKPEN

WITH CARE

A DELL PICTURE YEARLING

Published by
Dell Publishing
a division of
Bantam Doubleday Dell Publishing Group, Inc.
666 Fifth Avenue
New York, New York 10103

This work was first published in Great Britain in 1988
by Macmillan Children's Books.

ISBN: 0-440-40609-9
Reprinted by arrangement with Little, Brown and Company
Printed in the United States of America
April 1992

10 9 8 7 6 5 4 3 2 1

LBM

If I had a pig...

I would tell him...

...a joke.

I would hide from him...

...and jump out. Boo!

We could make a house…

...and have our friends sleep over.

We could paint pictures...

...of each other.

We could have fights…

...and piggybacks.

On his birthday...

...I would bake him a cake.

I would race him…

...to the park.

If it snowed…

...I would make him a snowpig.

We would need our boots...

...if it rained.

We could stay in the bath…

...until we wrinkled up.

I would read him a story...

...and take him to bed.